Kobi Takes Type 1 Diabetes to the Zoo

Written by
Kiona Dunn-Henegan
& Kobi Henegan

© Kiona Dunn-Henegan 2022

Copyright Material

Kobi Takes Type 1 Diabetes to the Zoo

Text copyright ©2022 by Kiona Dunn-Henegan. All rights reserved. No part of this book may be reproduced or transmitted in any form or by any means, electronic, or mechanical, including recording, or by any information storage and retrieval system, without written permission from the author, except by a reviewer who may quote brief passages in a review.

Interior and Cover Build by Infinity Flower Publishing, LLC
www.infinityflowerpublishing.com

ISBN 978-1-0879-0890-8 (Paperback)

Preface

Kobi Takes Type 1 Diabetes to the Zoo is based on the true story of Kobi Henegan.

What is Type 1?

Great question. I asked myself that very question when my son was diagnosed. Type 1 stands for Type 1 Diabetes (T1D) or juvenile diabetes. This series will take you on his journey and how we have managed our NEW NORMAL.

After his diagnosis, we had to adjust to our new normal. We had to manage Kobi's diabetes while staying positive. Finger pricks, counting carbs, creating new recipes, and administering injections became routine. Going to school, attending field trips, and vacations proved to be challenging at times. With the help of his family, Kobi and others in his village mastered managing his diabetes in all environments with a little planning.

Join Kobi, an elementary-aged boy from Georgia, who learns to navigate life with Type 1 Diabetes. Living with type 1 diabetes, a chronic illness can be very challenging, but the fun doesn't have to stop. This colorfully illustrated book details how Kobi manages his T1D while also having fun.

Kobi continues to inspire those around him with his positive attitude, tenacity and resilience. The support of family, friends, and daily affirmations keeps him positive and happy. Be sure to read the affirmations at the back of the book daily.

Dedication & Acknowledgements

This book is dedicated to all the Type 1 warriors, the moms and dads up at night checking numbers, the grandparents learning all over again, the aunties/uncles learning how to administer insulin, the brothers/sisters for your love, the cousins, and friends for all your support.

Thanks to the front office staff at the school, the nurse techs, the teachers, and administration. It takes a village.

Special thanks to Kobi, our very own warrior.

It was a lovely Friday morning in the Henegan home. Kobi woke up from sleeping and yawned. There were rays of light filtering into his room from the curtains. He sat up in bed and remembered he had a field trip to the zoo. Kobi has Type 1 Diabetes and everywhere that Kobi goes, his Type 1 Diabetes is sure to follow.

He quickly got down from his bed and went into the bathroom to prepare for the trip. His mother was one of the chaperones.

He brushed his teeth and took his bath. When he was done, he got dressed and took his bag to find his mom. He went to her bedroom.

"Good morning, Mom. I'm ready for my field trip with you and the rest of my classmates. I can't wait to see all the animals at the zoo. I am so excited!" he says while dancing around her bedroom.

She could hear the excitement in his voice. He was very anxious to leave. He wanted to get to the zoo. She was already dressed and just finished applying her makeup.

"Let's go to the kitchen, check your blood sugar levels, prepare breakfast, and take your insulin."

"Okay, Mom, I'll race you to the kitchen," Kobi said as he dashed downstairs. Once he arrived, he greeted his dad and sister with a happy hello!

He wanted to quickly eat his breakfast of delicious oatmeal, fruits, and juice, but Mom reminded him that they needed to check his levels. Kobi checked his levels by pricking his finger. His numbers were in range. Kobi's doctor reminded him to keep his blood sugar levels between 80 and 130mg.

Next, Mom reminded Kobi that for every 10 grams of carbs in food, he has to take 1 unit of insulin. Mom showed Kobi how to calculate his carb ratio. Mom said, "Oatmeal has 30 grams of carbs, fruits 18, and juice 15."

Kobi watched as his mom added 30+18+15 = 63. After adding, Mom reminded him they had to divide that number by 10. After calculating, Kobi needed 6.3 units of insulin before eating his breakfast.

Kobi loved going on field trips and new adventures. They got into Mom's car, and she drove to his school.

When they arrived, they met the children and parents lining up to enter the school bus. The children were very happy while their parents said hello to each other.

Kobi has Type 1 Diabetes and everywhere that Kobi goes, his Type 1 Diabetes is sure to follow.

When Kobi got on the bus he sat next to his mom. He was so excited; he could barely stop talking about seeing the elephant and the pandas.

When they arrived at the zoo, the children and their parents lined up at the gate to enter. They were each given a map and a zoo guide.

Kobi pointed at fun things he wanted to do on the map. He could not wait to get started.

A tour guide came to talk with the children, parents, and teachers.

"Welcome to the zoo. I am Ryan, your tour guide. I will take you around the zoo. I will show you each of the animal habitats and give you some facts about each one. I will also take you to the fun parts of the zoo. Feel free to ask me all the questions you may have. Are you ready to get started on the tour?" Ryan said.

"Yes! We are ready to start the tour," the children yelled.

The zoo had different habitats for different types of animals. There was a train in the zoo that travelled from one habitat to the other. Each habitat had signs, which contained facts about all the animals within. The zoo also featured an indoor and outdoor cafe, a large playground, a petting zoo, and a gift shop. Kobi has Type 1 Diabetes and everywhere that Kobi goes, his Type 1 Diabetes is sure to follow.

The children boarded the train happily with their parents and teachers. The tour guide took them from habitat to habitat. Ryan, the tour guide explained that a habitat is the home for plants and animals.

The first habitat they visited was the elephant habitat. "Elephants are the biggest land mammals. They are very interesting animals. They feed on plants. Those big things you see are tusks and they are made of ivory. They use their tusks for fighting and feeding. They are also the only animals with trunks. The trunks can be used to drink water and grip things," Ryan said.

"Wow, that's so interesting," Kobi said loudly.

Mom and Kobi stopped to check his blood sugar levels before moving onto the next habitat; his legs started to feel shaky. Kobi said, "Mom, my legs get shaky when my numbers are lower than what the doctor said it should be." His numbers were 100 and within range.

Kobi has Type 1 Diabetes and everywhere that Kobi goes, his Type 1 Diabetes is sure to follow.

They moved to the next habitat: Giraffes. They could see them feeding on leaves from treetops using their slender long necks.

"Mom, what do giraffes eat?" Kobi asked his mom.

"They eat fruits, shrubs, grass, and lettuce at the zoo," Kobi's mom said.

"Wow. That's amazing, Mom. I enjoyed the giraffes," he said happily.

The next stop was the giant panda habitat. They saw a small crowd taking pictures of the pandas. Kobi saw the pandas playing in their habitat, eating bamboo. "These are giant pandas. They originate from China. They are considered an endangered species. This means that very few of them are left in the whole world. We need to take good care of them. They eat plants, especially bamboo. Their coat is black and white," the tour guide explained.

Kobi was happy and loved seeing the pandas.

"Pandas are my favorite animals," Kobi said while dancing around.

Lastly, they visited the zebras and the bird habitats before lunch.

The children were hungry. The group walked to the café section of the zoo.

Kobi has Type 1 Diabetes and everywhere that Kobi goes, his Type 1 Diabetes is sure to follow.

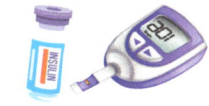

"Mom, Can I have pizza and juice?" Kobi asked.

"Yes, Kobi you can have pizza and juice. Do you remember how to calculate the insulin ratio for your meal like I taught you?"

"Yes, Mom. I receive one unit of insulin for every 10 grams of carbs I eat," Kobi answered.

"That's good, I am happy you remembered," she replied.

Kobi helped his mom find the carb count for the pizza. The count for the pizza was 70 grams of carbs for two slices. His juice was 10 grams of carbs. Kobi added 70+10=80. He then divided by 10 to get a total of 8 units of insulin.

"Great job," Mom said. Before eating, Mom and Kobi checked his blood sugar levels again and then he received 8 units of insulin for his food.

After they finished lunch, the tour guide took them to the petting zoo. This part of the zoo contained animals like pigs, goats, sheep, rabbits, and ponies. The children were allowed to feed and pet the animals. They had lots of fun feeding and playing with them.

The petting zoo was the only part where the children were allowed to come in close contact with the animals. Kobi and his classmates were allowed to play as much as they wanted.

Their last stop before leaving was the zoo gift shop. Each child was told to pick one item from the shop. Kobi picked a stuffed giant panda souvenir and showed his mom. Mom smiled and said, "Great choice, Kobi."

"Let's walk to the bus with the others," she said. They all got on the bus and went back to school. The children were happy. They had a wonderful time.

Kobi has Type 1 Diabetes and everywhere that Kobi goes, his Type 1 Diabetes is sure to follow.

When they arrived at school, Kobi dropped off his blood glucose meter, insulin, and extra snacks with the school nurse, Mrs. Tameka. She monitors his numbers and administers insulin at school daily.

"Thanks, Mrs. Tameka," Kobi said as he waved goodbye and went home with his mother.

Kobi has Type 1 Diabetes and everywhere that Kobi goes, his Type 1 Diabetes is sure to follow.

Look out for the next books in this series: *Kobi Takes Type 1 on Vacation* and *Our New Normal: Exploring My Emotions & Affirmations Journal*.

Also visit www.kobikonnects.org for more information

Words to know and Understand:

Our bodies are made up of **CELLS**.

TYPE 1 DIABETES is when your pancreas can't make insulin on its own.

INSULIN is a hormone made by beta cells in the pancreas. It allows sugar to enter the body's cell to give you energy.

The **PANCREAS** helps us get the energy we need from the food we eat.

It takes **ENERGY** in order to do work, think, and play.

HORMONES assist in our growing and changing.

An **ENDOCRINOLOGIST** is a doctor who specializes in hormones.

GLUCOSE is the main type of sugar in the blood and it gives energy to our cells.

Type 1 Diabetes Facts:

Type 1 Diabetes was once called insulin-dependent or juvenile diabetes. It usually develops in children, teens, and young adults, but it can happen at any age.

If you have Type 1 Diabetes, your pancreas doesn't make insulin or makes very little insulin. Type 1 Diabetes is thought to be caused by an autoimmune reaction (the body attacks itself by mistake) that stops your body from making insulin. If you have Type 1 Diabetes, you'll need to take insulin daily.

Currently, no one knows how to prevent Type 1 Diabetes and no cure has been developed yet. Research is promising and continues to change the lives of those living with Type 1 Diabetes. Type 1 Diabetes can be managed with the help of your endocrinologist and support.

SAYING POSITIVE THINGS TO YOURSELF CAN HELP YOU FEEL BETTER. PRACTICE SAYING THESE AFFIRMATIONS DAILY

Say these affirmations daily

I AM LOVED

I AM BRAVE

IT'S OKAY TO CRY

POSITIVE AFFIRMATIONS

I AM STRONG

I AM HAPPY

I AM SMART

CPSIA information can be obtained
at www.ICGtesting.com
Printed in the USA
LVHW072142181122
733281LV00002B/30